Up and Down

Monica Hughes
Illustrated by Beccy Blake

Rigby

Kate went on the swing.

5

Kate went on the merry-go-round.

7

"Dad," said Kate.
"Look at me! Look at me!"

8

9

Kate went up and down the slide.

11

13

Kate went on the big slide.
She went up, up, up.
She went down, down, down.

15

"Look at me!" said Kate.
"**Look at me!**" said Dad.